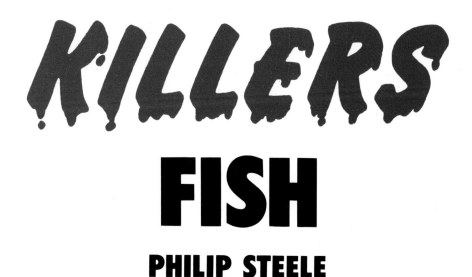

KILLERS

FISH

PHILIP STEELE

Julian Messner

Copyright © 1991 by Julian Messner

First published by Heinemann Children's Reference,
a division of Heinemann Educational Books Ltd
Original Copyright © 1991 Heinemann Educational Books Ltd

Published by Julian Messner, a division of
Silver Burdett Press, Inc., Simon & Schuster, Inc.
Prentice Hall Bldg., Englewood Cliffs, NJ 07632

JULIAN MESSNER and colophon are trademarks of
Simon & Schuster, Inc.

U.S. project editor: Nancy Furstinger

Printed in Hong Kong

Lib. ed. 10 9 8 7 6 5 4 3 2 1
Paper ed. 10 9 8 7 6 5 4 3 2 1

Library of Congress Cataloging-in-Publication Data
Steele, Philip.
 Killers: fish/by Philip Steele.
  p. cm.
 Summary: Discusses those underwater creatures that can be harmful
to humans, such as jellyfish, electric eels, and sharks.
 1. Dangerous fishes – Juvenile literature. 2. Poisonous fishes –
Juvenile literature. [1. Dangerous marine animals. 2. Poisonous
fishes]. I. Title.
 QL618.7.S74 1991
 597'.065-dc20

 ISBN 0-671-72239-5 (lib. ed.) ISBN 0-671-72240-9 (pbk.)

                                        89-77544
                                           CIP
                                            AC

Photographic acknowledgments
The author and publishers wish to acknowledge, with thanks, the following photographic sources:
a above *b* below *l* left *r* right
Cover photograph courtesy of Bruce Coleman/Francisco Erize
Ardea Photographics pp9 (Ian Beames), 11*a* (Nick Gordon); Camera Press p25*b*; Bruce Coleman pp11*b* (Francisco Erize), 19*a* (Norman Myers), 20*a* (Udo Hirsch), 21*b* (Roger Wilmshurst), 25*a* (Gunter Zeisler), 29 (M P L Fogden), 30*a* (Alain Compost), 31*a* (Christian Zuber), 31*b* (Peter Jackson); Matthew Hillier/Guinness Publishing, Courtesy of The Jane Marler Gallery, Salop p20*b*; Jacana p7*b* (Herve Chaumeton); Mansell Collection p15; National Medical Slide Bank p21*a*; NHPA pp4 (Anthony Bannister), p6 (James Carmichael), 7*a* (K H Switak), 10 (Martin Wendler), 12 (Philippa Scott), 13 (K H Switak), 14 (Anthony Bannister), 16*l* (K. Griffiths); 16*r* (James Carmichael), 17*a* (James Carmichael), 17*b* (Anthony Bannister), 18 (Anthony Bannister), 22 (Stephen Dalton), 23*a* (K H Switak), 28 (R J Erwin); Planet Earth Pictures p30*b* (Richard Matthews); Topham p23*b*.
The publishers have made every effort to trace the copyright holders, but if they have inadvertently overlooked any, they will be pleased to make the necessary arrangement at the first opportunity.

CONTENTS

DANGER UNDERWATER

A NIMALS kill and are killed. This is a fact of nature. Many fish eat plankton — the tiny creatures and plants that drift in the oceans. Smaller fish are eaten by larger fish. Animals kill only to stay alive, however, or to defend themselves when attacked.

When we humans enter the sea, we may be injured or killed by many underwater creatures.

Mako shark

Who's who underwater?

This book is about creatures that live underwater. It does not discuss marine mammals, such as whales, which must come to the surface to breathe, or reptiles, such as crocodiles and sea snakes. The first creatures to be discussed are coelenterates, such as sea anemones and jellyfish. They can be dangerous stingers.

Like coelenterates, mollusks, such as octopuses, also have soft bodies. Some, like the cone shell, may be protected by an outer shell. The larger mollusks, such as cuttlefish, may have a bony plate inside their bodies instead of a shell.

The fish in this book belong to two main groups. The sharks and rays have skeletons made of a hard material called cartilage. The other fish have skeletons made of bone.

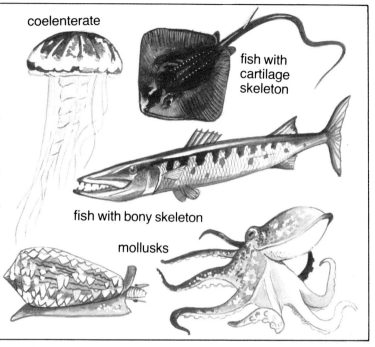

coelenterate

fish with cartilage skeleton

fish with bony skeleton

mollusks

 We don't know how many people are killed by water creatures. As many as 1,000 may be killed by sharks each year. Many more people are injured by other fish.

A KILLER'S WEAPON

O VER the ages, many water creatures have developed weapons. Octopuses have arms, or tentacles, with suckers on them that grip and poison their victims. Crustaceans, such as crabs and lobsters, have pincers. Many fish have spines, armor plating, or sharp teeth. Some can even give an electric shock!

Red fiddler crab

DEATH ON THE TIDE

YOU may see a swarm of jellyfish when you are swimming. You might also see some washed up on a beach. Stay away from them! Although they are mostly made up of water, their bodies and tentacles can sting you. Jellyfish sting to catch prey and to defend themselves. As they bob in the water, the see-through lumps of "jelly" throb, and their tentacles trail behind them.

SEA WASPS

THE most dangerous jellyfish of all are found in the Indian and Pacific oceans. Some types of these, known as sea wasps, are as poisonous as deadly snakes like the cobra. Sea wasps have tentacles up to 23 feet long, that are armed with powerful stingers. Once victims have been stung, they start to sweat, shake, lose their sight, and choke. They may die within minutes.

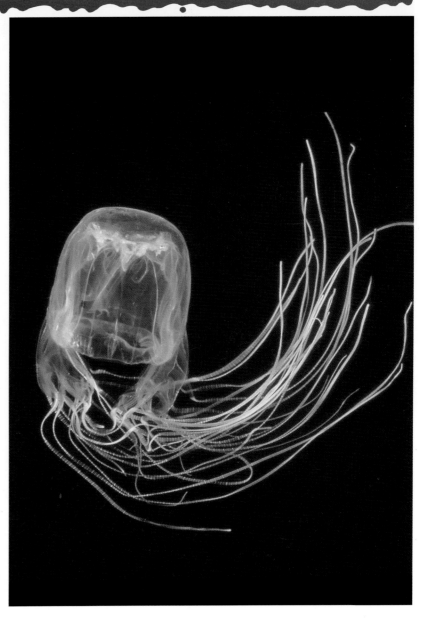

Sea wasp

8

THE FLOWERS OF EVIL

S EA anemones may look like beautiful marine plants, but they are animals that can sting. The most poisonous live in the Pacific Ocean, near Samoa. There, people cook and eat them. However, if people eat these animals raw or not properly cooked, they can die.

THE MAN-O'-WAR

T HE Portuguese man-o'-war is a relative of the jellyfish. It is about 12 inches long and 6 inches across. Battleships were once called men-o'-war, and this deadly coelenterate was named after them. It moves along on the waves by means of a large float. It is very dangerous because of its half a million stingers. When its tentacles brush against something, barbed threads uncoil from them. The barbs strike the victim's skin and inject venom, a poisonous form of saliva. The victim feels sick and giddy and may become paralyzed. Small children and weak adults may die. The shock of a man-o'-war attack might make even a strong swimmer drown.

Portuguese man-o'-war

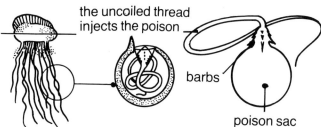
the uncoiled thread injects the poison

barbs

poison sac

POISON IN PARADISE

shell

eye

foot

harpoon

SEASHELLS are often very beautiful, and many people collect them. However, the finely patterned cone-shell creatures of the Indian and Pacific oceans are best left alone. All species are dangerous, and some are deadly. Victims feel numb, their vision blurs, and they become paralyzed.

The secret of the cone shells' weapon system is a poison gland. It pumps venom through a tube to hollow harpoons that tear at the victim's skin.

Marble cone

THE CURSE OF THE MUMMIES

O NE tiny water snail is a link in a terrible chain of disease. The disease is called bilharzia. It is caused by a tiny fluke worm. The larva of the worm lives in the snail, which breeds in lakes and rivers in tropical Africa and South America. When the worm grows into an adult, it leaves the snail. It enters the body of an animal or human who bathes in the water. The fluke worm can damage the brain, lungs, and other organs.

★ **More than 200 million people have bilharzia. Examinations of Egyptian mummies show it was common long ago, too.**

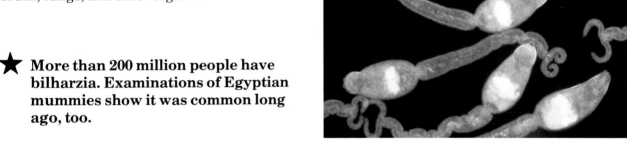

THE GIANT-CLAM MYSTERY

C ONE shells and water snails both have single shells. Many mollusks have double shells joined by a hinge. They are called bivalves. The largest bivalve is the giant clam. It can be more than 3 feet across and weigh 600 pounds. Some people claim it can kill humans by trapping a diver's arm or leg. The diver cannot escape from the clam's tight grip and drowns. However, there is no proof this has ever happened. A clam closes its shell slowly, so a diver can normally escape in time.

Giant clam on the Great Barrier Reef, Australia

11

TENTACLES OF TERROR

T HE giant squid is the largest mollusk of all. Its eyes are larger than the eyes of any other animal. There have been tales of monster squids more than 65 feet long. However, the largest one found in recent years was 46 feet long. Squids are blue-blooded. They travel backward by taking in water and squirting it out. They have eight arms and two long tentacles covered with suckers that grip prey. They can escape from danger by squirting a cloud of black liquid into the water.

Squids have venom glands that are used to stun prey. They use their beaklike mouth to kill fish by biting them through the back.

The Kraken comes to life

Legends tell of sea monsters with many arms that dragged sailors to a watery grave. The people of Norway called them Krakens. In the last century, scientists in Denmark examined a huge creature washed up on a beach. It was not a Kraken. It was a giant squid.

THE PARALYZERS

O CTOPUSES look scary. They have eight wiggling arms covered with suckers. These mollusks also produce venom that paralyzes and kills their prey. They hide in crevices in the rocks, and many have scared divers or fishermen by gripping their arm or leg. However, they usually do not harm people.

The most dangerous octopuses are not the biggest. The blue-ringed or spotted octopuses of the Indian and Pacific oceans are only 6 inches across. However, they have a powerful venom. It is squirted into the victims when the octopuses bite. The victims feel sick, lose their speech and sight, and become paralyzed. They may die unless they are rushed to the hospital.

Blue-ringed octopus

THE SHARKS

OST fish have a buoyancy tank inside their bodies that keeps them afloat. Sharks have none. If they do not keep swimming, they will sink and die.

There are 300 species of sharks. Some are small and harmless. The two largest species, the whale shark and the basking shark, eat only plankton. Other species are flesh-eaters. Only 27 species attack people, but that is enough to make us fear them. Some sharks, such as the Greenland, have poisonous flesh.

Ten top terrors

1 Great white shark	6 Mako shark
2 Tiger shark	7 Lemon shark
3 Dusky shark	8 Grey nurse shark
4 Bull shark	9 Sand shark
5 Hammerhead shark	10 Reef white-tip shark

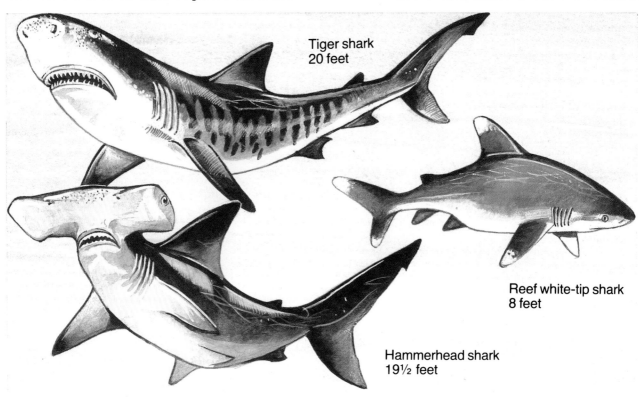

Tiger shark
20 feet

Reef white-tip shark
8 feet

Hammerhead shark
19½ feet

TEETH OF TERROR

A SHARK'S wide, curved mouth is packed with several rows of razor-sharp teeth. The teeth at the rear move forward to replace the front ones as they wear out. The teeth may be replaced every 10 days. Sharks have powerful jaws and teeth that slant backward. It is impossible for the victim to get free.

Sharks may attack anything that moves. They seem to be attracted by certain kinds of motion in the water. However, other movements scare them off. Sharks are believed to have a fine sense of hearing and smell. They can scent a drop of blood from far away.

Lemon shark

TELLTALE FINS

S HARKS are all very strong swimmers. They balance, steer, and move by means of their powerful fins and curved tail.

15

THE GREAT WHITE SHARK

T HE great white shark is the world's largest flesh-eating fish. The female is larger than the male. It is usually about 14 feet long and weighs 1,550 pounds. Some of the largest are more than twice as long and three times as heavy. Most sharks need to live in seas with a temperature of more than 70°F. The great white shark will search for large prey in much cooler waters.

Some people hate killers such as the great white shark. However, these creatures have simply adapted to a life of hunting in order to live. The great white shark has adapted so well that it has survived for hundreds of millions of years.

Spot the shark

If you look behind the head of most kinds of fish, you will see a bony flap on each side. Fish obtain the oxygen they need to stay alive directly from water that is taken in through the mouth. The water moves back out of the fish through the flaps, which cover organs called gills. Sharks have many slits instead of single, bony flaps.

Most fish are covered with flat scales. Shark skin is covered with tiny ridges that look like teeth. Their teeth are really larger versions of the same ridges.

Galapagos shark

The great white shark eats fish and squid. It also hunts dolphins, sea lions, seals, and turtles. It may tear chunks of flesh from the victims or swallow them whole. Entire human bodies have been found in the stomachs of sharks.

SHARK ATTACK!

SHARKS are the most aggressive of all sea creatures. They are never afraid, and some species will attack a boat full of people. When they are hunting, little will stand in their way. Bathers in dangerous areas should always be careful.

Some popular movies have played upon people's fears of being attacked by sharks. However, the chances of being killed by one are slim. In fact, sharks are in more danger from humans than humans are from sharks. Some people kill them simply for sport.

Shark-infested seas

Most shark attacks occur in the northwest Atlantic, off the Pacific coast of North America, in the Indian Ocean, and off the coasts of Japan, Australia, and southern Africa. Sometimes, there are shark attacks in the Mediterranean Sea. The map shows where swimmers are in the greatest danger of attack.

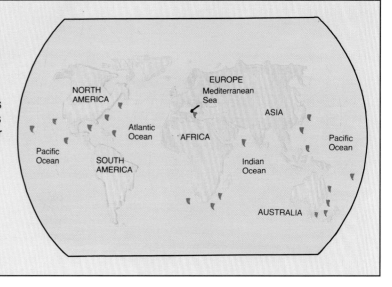

STAYING SAFE

S HARKS prefer warm seas, and so do tourists. Some of the most popular beaches are located near shark-infested waters. Because great white sharks may come close to shore, it is essential to protect these places. Nets often are placed across the entrance to a bay or beach to prevent the sharks from coming ashore.

TEETH LIKE DAGGERS

WHEN barracuda are young, they swim in shoals, or large groups. When they are older, they hunt alone among coral reefs. The largest species, the great barracuda, is a bony fish almost 8 feet long. Its body is shaped like a torpedo and its powerful jaws hold a set of very sharp teeth. Barracuda often herd their prey together before eating them.

Barracuda are found in both the Pacific and Atlantic oceans, and in the Mediterranean Sea.

The most aggressive ones seem to be in the Caribbean Sea. Divers fear them. The barracuda appear suddenly. Then, mistaking the metal on the divers' equipment for prey, they may attack.

Barracuda

DIVERS AT RISK

THE coral reefs of the tropics are home to other dangerous fish. There are 120 species of moray eels. The biggest is more than 9 feet long.

Moray eels hide in crevices in the rocks. If prey, such as a starfish, comes too near, the eel darts out and gulps it down whole. Moray eels have a set of razor-sharp teeth. If one is threatened, it can turn vicious. Divers injured by an eel must get help fast.

 Eating moray eels may kill people.

GREEDY EATERS

M OST animals kill only what they can eat. The bluefish is an exception. It can kill ten times as many fish as it can eat. At times it vomits up its catch and starts killing again.

The bluefish is about 16 inches in length. Huge shoals of bluefish are found in many warm seas. In the summer, there may be a billion of them off the eastern coast of the United States. Bluefish eat menhaden, mackerel, herring, and mullet.

Hungry shoals of bluefish have been known to injure swimmers. However, there is no evidence that anyone was ever killed by bluefish.

CHOPPER MOUTHS

I N the rivers of the South American jungle live the world's fiercest freshwater fish. There are 18 species of piranha. Only four of these are believed to be dangerous to humans. The red piranha, which is about 12 inches long, is the most feared. It swims rapidly and uses its terrifying teeth to chop up prey.

Red piranha

LIVING PREY

P IRANHAS hunt in shoals of thousands. Just the scent of blood or the struggles of a drowning animal may attract large numbers of them. They will eat the flesh of any creature. A large mammal, such as a horse, might be eaten by them in a few minutes.

There are many cases of humans being attacked by piranhas. There are, however, no reliable records of people being killed by them.

SHOCKERS!

MORE than 100 species of fish can produce electricity. They have organs that operate like batteries. They may use these to stun prey, to defend themselves, or to help them navigate. A few can give people a bad shock.

There are more than 30 species of electric rays, or torpedo rays. They have flat, disk-shaped bodies, and skeletons made of cartilage, like those of sharks. The largest are almost 6 feet long. There are two large electric units inside a ray's body, on either side of the head. The prey may be wrapped in the ray's fins and stunned by them. Electric rays can give out between 40 and 220 volts of electricity.

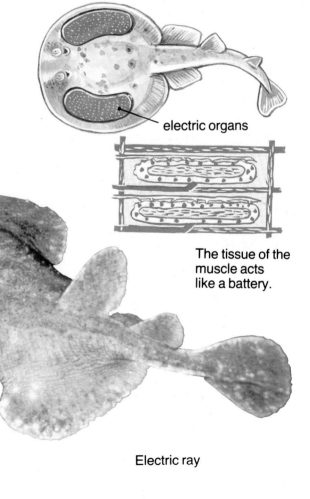

electric organs

The tissue of the muscle acts like a battery.

Electric ray

THE ELECTRIC EEL

T HE electric eel is so named because it can produce electricity and because, like eels, it is long and thin. It is actually related to the knife-fishes rather than to the true eels. It lives in rivers and lakes in South America. The electric eel has electric organs running from behind its head to the end of its tail. It is the most powerful electric fish. It gives out a shock of between 400 and 650 volts. The electric current in a house is only 120 volts.

ELECTRIC CATFISH

T HE lakes and rivers of Africa are home to the electric catfish. It feeds on creatures that live in the mud. The whiskery feelers around its mouth locate prey. Its back and tail muscles act as electric units, giving out between 50 and 350 volts.

POISONOUS FISH

A NIMALS that use fangs or spines to inject poison into their victims are said to be venomous. Weever fishes of the Atlantic Ocean and the Mediterranean have spiny dorsal, or back, fins. In the summer, they are often half-buried in sand. If a swimmer steps on one, he or she is injected with venom.

Sting rays have flattened bodies between 1 and 15 feet wide, and long tails. A spine on the tail can strike out in defense. It can cut into the flesh and inject venom. Both weever and sting ray attacks are terribly painful and can bring sudden death to victims with weak hearts.

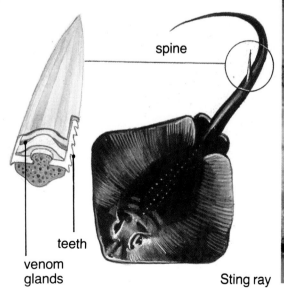

spine

teeth

venom glands

Sting ray

THE STING

T HERE are about 250 species of scorpion fish. They are named after the stinging scorpions of the desert. Like them, these fish can also deliver a fatal sting. The most dangerous are three species known as stonefish. They live in the Indian and Pacific oceans. Stonefish are the most venomous fish in the sea. Their poison usually is injected by means of 13 spines on the fish's fins. It often causes death.

Stonefish

THE DEADLY PUFFERS

T HE tiger puffer fish of the East China Sea is covered with spines. It can blow its body up to twice its normal size to scare away enemies. Its organs contain one of the deadliest natural poisons known. Someone eating a puffer stands a 60 percent chance of dying. There is no known antidote.

★ **The puffer is highly valued in Japan as food! The poisonous parts are removed, and the fish is served as a dish called *fugu*. It takes ten years to learn to be a *fugu* chef.**

27

ON THE OCEAN FLOOR

NE group of sea creatures is known as echinoderms. These include sea urchins and starfish. Sea urchins are round and covered with spines. If you step on one, it can hurt very much. If you step on a venomous one, such as the diadem of the Caribbean Sea, you may receive a very bad wound. The worst of all is a sea urchin of the Indian and Pacific oceans called *Toxopneustes pileolus*. If its spines prick you, you may be paralyzed or even killed.

One starfish might be called a killer for another reason. The crown-of-thorns starfish, of the Indian and Pacific oceans, eats the living parts of coral in large amounts. It has destroyed great areas of Australia's Great Barrier Reef. When the coral reefs die, the edible fish that normally live around them leave. When the fish leave people may go hungry.

Sea urchins

Crown-of-thorns starfish

MENACES OF THE DEEP

OW deep is the ocean? At one point the Pacific is 36,192 feet deep. As a diving bell goes deeper, the ocean gets darker, until there is no light.

Humans visiting the ocean depths would not be in danger from the creatures living there. Most of them are very small. Some of them make their own light, giving off an eerie glow. The viperfish has long curving fangs tipped with barbs. The dragonfish is also toothy. The gulper has huge jaws and an expandable belly. The deep-sea hatchet fish has very sharp vision. The angler fish has a light dangling in front of its large jaws that lures prey to almost certain death.

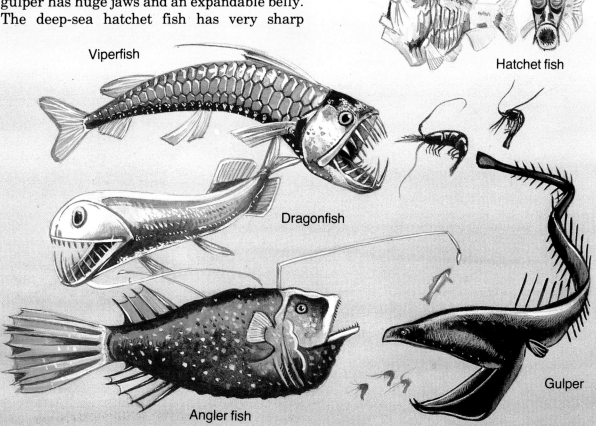

Viperfish

Hatchet fish

Dragonfish

Gulper

Angler fish

29

SAVING WATER CREATURES

MANY kinds of water-dwelling creatures are now in danger because of human activities. For example, large numbers of them are killed simply for sport. Also, if too many fish of one species are caught, the species may become scarce. And the creatures that eat them may become scarce, too.

When oil tankers are wrecked at sea, thick oil may leak out and cover entire coasts, killing plants, fish, and sea birds. Dumping garbage, sewage, and chemical waste into rivers and seas destroys plant and animal life. The waters around nuclear-power plants can also be poisoned by radioactive materials. Coating hulls of ships with chemicals that kill weeds can poison mollusks. Draining creeks, inlets, and lakes for farming can leave water creatures without homes. Chemicals used in farming may also drain into streams and rivers, killing fish. Many people want to limit or control the activities that lead to these problems. That would certainly help. Since we humans created many of the problems, we also can solve them.

The future of the oceans

Between the years 1990 and 2090, the population of the world may double. The oceans may be needed as a vital resource. They can provide us with food. We may even be able to farm the seabed. However, right now, we are poisoning our seas and destroying our supply of fish.

What can **you** do? Support organizations that want a cleaner, better environment and an end to the needless killing of wildlife.

Let us hope that 100 years from now the seas will still be the home of all the great creatures of the deep.

Sea creatures at risk from human activities

★ Marine turtles
★ Manatees
★ Whales
★ Dolphins
★ Seals
★ Sea birds
★ Sea otters
★ Fish

INDEX